CRYSTALLINE

A Waterlore Romance

Riona Beck

For those of you reclaiming what is yours.

Table of Contents

Author's Note

Please be aware, dear reader, that you are not diving into a deeply researched, highly accurate historical novel. My points of interest derived primarily from the Enclosure Acts of the 18th and 19th centuries, and my efforts to explore the subject could hardly be called scholarly. If you find anything especially egregious, you are welcome to inform me of it kindly, if you so desire. Otherwise, please enjoy this story that is meant to be a short, romantic diversion (complete with a book boyfriend who cooks breakfast).

Chapter 1

Ella was a proper young woman. She was devoted to maintaining propriety even while working outside in late summer's heat, which meant staying fully clothed while clearing the overgrowth and debris crowding the pond on her family property.

The water sparkled in the sunlight, throwing diamonds into Ella's eyes. It was so beautiful it might have been an enchantment. The woods behind the pond were said to be full of fairies and spirits who could cast such enchantments. These spirits were wicked, sly creatures who lay in wait for unwary humans. Such humans, when they stumbled into such hiding places, would find their virtue in grave danger, or their most cherished memory, or even their life.

And so Ella, wiping sweat from her round, flushed face, refused to gaze longingly at the cool, dark depths of the water, refused to loosen even one button on her faded yellow gown. Her strong, plump arms continued uprooting the plants that choked the mouth of the little stream which fed these enticing and roguishly sparkling waters.

"I would have come to help you earlier," Ella said to the pond, "but you understand how

Stepmother is. I have been polishing silver as though the king were coming to visit. Quite pointless, really."

The pond said nothing, of course. But it must have been taking its roguishness rather seriously that day. For when Ella was engaged with a particularly stubborn weed, whether by magic or misfortune—or ancient shoes which really should have been replaced years ago—she slipped, lost her grip on the weed, and tumbled into the pond.

It was cold and startling and refreshing. Her eyes opened of their own accord—and widened in surprise. The pond was a vast cavern stretching around and below her, its depths far more expansive than the surface of it had suggested, though they disappeared into darkness and plant life. It was the most wonderful view—until Ella remembered that she did not know how to swim.

This took approximately one second.

She thrashed and struggled, but the surface was far beyond her reach. Panic began to catch at her throat and lungs. Her limbs struggled for purchase in vain. Then something caught her round the waist and held her tight. She screamed, inviting the pond into her lungs, and thrashed blindly until darkness claimed her.

She awoke, choking and coughing. When she had expelled the last of the pond water, drawing in ragged gasps of air, Ella struggled to sit upright.

"I'm flattered by your sense of urgency," said a low male voice. Strong arms encircled her, supporting her and keeping her from sitting upright. "I would have brought you myself, however, if you had waited."

A pale man was smiling down at her. Ella blinked and stared in a way that surely ignored propriety altogether. The sharp planes of his face, as angular as hers was round, made him almost severe looking, but his smile was smooth and disarming. When he shifted slightly his skin shimmered a pale blue. This startling fact was overshadowed by the fact that he still held her. Ella had had no such intimate contact with a man before. It should have been appalling. She should remove herself. But Ella had no wish to leave the stranger's embrace. There was far too little fabric between her skin and his, which felt good in a way she feared might be bad and warmed her instantly.

"Thank you for rescuing me," she croaked. "It was clumsy of me to fall in."

"Most of my visitors dive in gracefully, but I have seen a few cannonball their way down." He grinned. "You may be the first to fall."

He made it sound like a compliment, as if he were in no hurry to let her go. Ella wished she could stay where she was indefinitely, yet could no longer pretend she did not know he held her;

return to propriety she must. But it seemed terribly boring.

"I seem to have lost my dress," she said.

"Wet clothes have a way of dragging one down, in my experience. I removed it. It is hanging up by the fire, there, drying." The stranger nodded his head and Ella followed the movement, catching a glimpse of her surroundings as she did so. They appeared to be in a cozy, small sitting room. The fire in the fireplace blazed, and a familiar faded yellow dress hanging from a wooden rack steamed next to it. An assortment of luxurious if somewhat faded chaise lounges adorned the room. But the stranger cradled Ella on a soft rug of blues and greens. *That must explain the blue tinge to his skin,* Ella told herself. And why, despite being in only her damp stays, chemise, and drawers, she felt as comfortable as one could expect–and entirely bothered in other ways.

"Now we must get you somewhere more comfortable," said the stranger in a caressing voice, which just went to show that even handsome, dashing men did not read minds. Instead of releasing her, he drew her closer until her breath stirred the simple white shirt he wore. The hollow at his throat made Ella's own throat go dry. With one finger he lifted her chin until he caught her gaze. "The afternoon is ours, love."

Ella could only stare. She felt no fear, only surprise and a strange hunger deep in her belly. The pale man smiled.

"How would you be pleasured?" He asked in liquid tones. His eyes glanced from her face to her barely-covered breasts, to the space between her legs as he spoke, and a light kindled his gaze that seemed to tingle across her skin. "Hot and desperate? To be taken roughly until I steal your voice. Shall I ravish you?" A languid hand drawn up Ella's thigh elicited a gasp. He drew away as she pulled her knees instinctively towards her chest.

"No? I should have guessed not. A tender creature such as yourself requires a certain gentleness. Let me bring you to pleasure slowly."

"I—well, what I mean—what are you talking about?" Ella gasped, pressing a hand lightly to his chest. His skin was cool and smooth through the shirt, making her want to drag her palm from shoulder to shoulder, preferably without said shirt in the way. But his large hand caught hers and stilled the motion.

"You mean to say," he said, his pale blue eyes peering into hers, "you did not come here for me to make love to you?" A new thought must have struck him, for his eyes widened and he leaned away. "Do you know what making love means?"

"Yes. Of course," Ella said. Her cheeks colored. "Um, a little. I have seen sheep couple and my stepmother told me, um, some things." She frowned. Stepmother's description was unexciting and awkward at best, frightening at worst. But the way this stranger made her body respond hadn't brought to mind that brief discussion, if discussion it could be called. Rather, it had driven everything from her mind and stirred things in her body that she had only felt briefly before. She wanted more.

But the stranger's brows drew together in worry. He released her, laying her back on the rug, and stood.

"I do not seduce virgins," he said sternly.

Ella sat upright and frowned, blinking up at him. "Couldn't you make an exception for me?"

"I see. You fell in, not knowing I was here. You were not looking for me at all."

"Where is here, exactly?"

Without explanation, the man scooped her into his arms and strode across the room. Ella cried out in surprise at this sudden removal, though she felt no desire to escape his arms or the way he cradled her ample body with ease.

"Women come to me understanding what they ask for," he said. "They don't understand how capably I fulfill their requests."

"Oh." Understanding dawned. "You are a prostitute."

"I prefer *nymph de l'eau*. Your kind call me water spirit, but I assure you, I am very much a physical being. It is against my nature to pleasure unsuspecting intruders, especially those who don't understand the most rudimentary elements of love-making."

"You could show me," she said, to her own surprise. "Surely you can do that?"

He gazed at her. "I could do more than that," he said, his voice liquid once again. "I could do so much more—but no. I will see you to the edge of the pond."

Now she felt embarrassed and even more confused than before, despite the stranger clarifying his occupation—or perhaps because of that. "Put me down," she insisted. "I will walk."

"Darling, this is the home of Rodan the lover," said the stranger. "You'll have to swim."

Chapter 2

He set her down in a coolly lit entryway. The weather had turned stormy, but Ella could not hear anything. She squinted through the window. She could not see the bank. She could not see much of anything, in fact, because–

"We're underwater," she said, and gulped. "When you said swim, I thought you meant across the pond, not through it."

Rodan pulled something from a basket woven of green reeds and held it out to show her. It looked like a pearl, small and iridescent. "This will allow you to breathe until you reach the shore," he explained. "However, as you found me by accident, I am inclined not to give it to you. You might start a habit of taking strange things from strange men."

"I'll do no such thing," Ella replied. "You saved me from drowning and refused to make love to me. As there is nothing else for it, I would rather not need you to rescue me again." Still proper, she held out her hand and waited for the item.

"Suit yourself." Rodan placed the pearl in her hand and indicated she was to swallow it. "The effects will last long enough for your journey."

It went down her throat like a soft piece of ice, leaving a little trail of cold in her throat. Rodan was opening the door. He took her hand, and led her through.

Ella noted the pocket of air surrounding the open door, which held just room enough for the two of them. His arms encircled her once more. But she had not time to revel in this, for he propelled them through the bubble and into the water.

It was a rush of cold silk against her skin, running cool fingers through her hair. She managed to keep her eyes open and found it easy as anything. The blue water cleared so that she could see quite well, and the surroundings enchanted her. Schools of silver fish darted beneath them like low scudding clouds into tiny forests of graceful water weeds. They ascended quickly, the engulfing water flow changing direction, and crowds of taller water plants rose up in the distance like a vast forest. The house fell away behind them, quickly swallowed in a murky dusk, until the faint yellow glow of the windows might have been the eyes of some dreadful creature. Ella shuddered.

"You should see it when the water is at her clearest," said Rodan, nodding ahead. A fine netting on his neck–gills, she realized with surprise–fluttered delicately. Ella tore her gaze away and looked where he indicated. Above them, a grey pallor spread across the water like a film of dust. The water looked ill.

"Is this where the stream feeds it?" She asked, forgetting to be surprised that she could speak underwater, let alone breathe. The water tickled her mouth and skin. Reaching a hand up, she murmured in surprise to find a delicate fluttering on her neck.

"Yes." A grim light entered Rodan's eyes. "I cannot leave the water, or I would clean it myself."

"I will clean it," Ella said. "I was cleaning it, before I fell in."

"Were you?" He glanced at her in surprise. "How considerate of the spirits you must be."

Not knowing until minutes ago that spirits lived in the pond, Ella only responded, "I love this place. Above the surface, that is."

"And above the surface is where you must stay." Rodan turned her to face him. "It was a delight to meet you, love. Have a pleasant life."

And suddenly Ella found herself sitting on the bank, sopping wet.

How odd everything looked now that she had seen the pond from beneath the surface. A fairy world at that. Or rather, a spirit world, and she hadn't lost a thing. She decided the word spirit suited Rodan better. Despite his being, as he had said, very corporeal, it was the word he had used.

Marveling, she glanced around her. The sun was lower in the sky, meaning it was almost time for tea. She felt as though the sun ought to be higher, or in the very same place, or maybe a different color; a strange event to mark her strange adventure. But everything looked as it always had at the pond gracing the very edge of the late baronet's land.

The stream still needed tending, but she hadn't time for that. She would have to come back tomorrow. Ella had cleared the stream every few years to allow for the pond to remain clear, but it seemed a much more interesting task now that thoughts of a handsome, roguish water spirit stirred within her as it stirred in the cool depths.

"His manners are extremely confusing," she announced to no one, "but I suppose, for a spirit, he could have been worse."

Rodan watched her leave below the surface of the water, out of sight. His thoughts were a tangle of roots and water. He should not have slipped another pearl into her bodice, practically inviting her to return. Many humans had visited him in his current abode, but this one whose name he did not even know tugged at him like the waves at low tide.

How alluring she was, with her round, generous curves, her large brown eyes, her hair golden and shining! He found her simplicity refreshing, unexpected; women were coy with him, men were sometimes embarrassed to go to him. But this stranger was so honest. *And demanding*, he thought. He grinned a grin that made all of his clients weak in the knees. *I'd like to get on my knees for her–*

"*No*, Rodan." He scrubbed his face violently. He'd meant what he said about her staying on land. He had good reason to say it and to believe it, to refuse to give her what everyone came to him for. He felt the weight of this reason on his shoulders every day. It rested on his shoulders the way dis-ease rested on the water's surface.

There was nothing else for it. *Time for a good, stiff– er, sobering drink*, he told himself, and swam home swiftly.

Chapter 3

For once, Ella was thankful that her bedroom was on the ground floor and that the window never fully shut. She tumbled inside and scrambled to snatch her second gown from its peg on the wall. It was a sad thing of faded pink, but at least she could dress herself in it without the help of a servant. She dressed in a hurry and wrung out her wet hair through the open window, peering towards the pond. She couldn't see it from there.

She did, however, remember her dress, still warming itself beside Rodan's sitting room fire. She'd lost something after all, though through forgetfulness rather than a spirit's wiles.

What if he did it on purpose so I must go back? She thought wistfully. But he had told her to stay on land. *Even still.*

"I shall have to get it back," she said aloud.

"Ella! Ella, to whom are you speaking, girl? Get out here at once! I have been calling you for ages!" Stepmother's sharp voice accompanied a rapping on the door. Ella banged her head on the window as she drew inside. When she opened her door, the older woman's eyes blazed with righteous anger.

"Finally! Ella, our distinguished guest arrives soon, and I–good gracious! Ella, what on earth have you been doing? No, don't tell me." Stepmother lifted a scented handkerchief to her nose and shut her eyes. "Why must you go near that horrid pond? Don't you have the sense to realize that a wicked fairy might find you? Or worse, one of those dirty, itinerant families?"

"How might they be worse?" Ella asked, but Stepmother ignored her and went on about the state of the meal and how real baronetcies always observed proper meal times.

"Just hurry and come to the kitchen at once," she finished.

"The cake is ready, Stepmother, and I'll finish the sandwiches and come right back to my room," Ella said, "just as we discussed." *And then I can retrieve my dress before you notice it's gone, and maybe see if he...*

"You'll do no such thing, girl. Have you lost your wits?" Stepmother's voice jolted her from the beginnings of a delicious daydream. "Finish the meal and bring it to the parlor, where you will wait, just as we discussed."

Ella bit her lip to keep from saying that they had discussed no such thing, as that would get her nowhere. She was used to serving the food in her older dress to keep up the pretense that they still kept servants; the baronetess never received visitors for Ella, and when she received the few of her own acquaintance, always said that her stepdaughter was out shopping with friends or ill in her room. But to stay with the guests was different. And different circumstances or not, asking questions of Stepmother never got her anywhere.

And so, half an hour later, Ella found herself, damp hair arranged in a tidy, braided bun, seated across from the distinguished guest, one Sir Edward. He was a portly man about twice her age. He kept sneaking mean little smiles at her over his port glass and dropping crumbs into his beard while Stepmother babbled on as gaily as a parrot.

"Ella, my dear, do show Sir Edward the garden. I'm afraid my head aches, and you did promise him a walk."

"I'm afraid I did not," Ella began, but her stepmother's face turned pink and pinched, and Sir Edward had already stood and offered his arm. He looked so like a dog hoping for a bone that Ella almost pitied him. Almost.

"Oh. Very well." She begrudgingly took his arm and went towards the door, as her stepmother twittered and chirped about what a lovely day it was and how much the exercise would be good for her, and be sure to be a charming hostess for dear Sir Edward!

The afternoon was warm, but a small breeze made it less oppressive. Ella could have almost enjoyed the walk but for two things. One, she kept thinking about how much more invigorating a swim would feel, and how wonderful it would be to touch Rodan's skin again. There was a danger and an allure to him which haunted her, dragging her thoughts down avenues she had scarce ventured before and making her wish she could flee to the pond again. Secondly, Sir Edward kept chuckling as if something funny had happened, until she could no longer ignore him.

"You seem very distracted, Miss Ella," he said. His voice was oily and heavy, and Ella heard the beginnings of a wheeze. *He should probably see a doctor,* she thought. *Poor man.* The poor man patted her arm with a sweaty hand. "But fret not. I have been told I make a lovely proposal of marriage."

Ella looked at him, astonished. "By whom? Have you proposed to many people?"

"Why," he faltered, looking puzzled, "yes. All my wives. Good women, proper wives, but sadly all dead. But I shall not be alone for long."

"I'm sure Stepmother will be honored," Ella replied archly. "Though you should probably ask her instead of walking out here with me."

"Oh, my dear." He laughed, a sound which made Ella cringe. "Clever little thing, but not too clever! Your virtues are numerous. Why would I want that old bag? When you and I are married, she will get enough money to suit her, but you are the real prize."

Ella withdrew her arm in shock. "Me! But that is ridiculous. Why," she fumbled, grasping for an escape from this nightmarish comedy, "we have only just met!"

"That does not signify! Besides, I've seen you serving food many times. Your charade does not fool me, Miss Ella. I know the shabbily-disguised poverty in which you live. As my wife you will live in comfort and dignity. And you shall lack no pleasure you desire," he continued, his face oozing into a leer. "I have also been told that I am as skilled at love-making as the god Eros himself."

"Get away!" Ella cried. "I will not marry you, even if you asked me! Which you haven't!"

In such a state of distraction and distress, she couldn't remember running all the way to the pond. When she bent over to catch her breath, something small slipped from her bodice and landed in the grass, glinting in the sun. It was one of Rodan's pearls. Ella chose not to consider too closely how it got there. Without a second thought, she swallowed the pearl, stripped off her dress—and shoes, this time—and jumped from the bank.

Chapter 4

Oh, gloriously cold water! How much more welcome this time it was. Ella gulped in lungfuls. Without the threat of drowning, she could marvel at the pond at length. Even with the ability to swim, she should have been frightened as she sank into the gloomy, jewel-toned depths. But she merely glanced around her in wonder until the twin glow of windows came into view. Thrashing and struggling, she managed to get hold of some tall, willowy plants near the front door. Then she grappled her way to the air bubble and let herself in.

Her feet left damp footprints on the hard floor. The house was silent, but the warmth greeted her pleasantly as she took in the surroundings. There was a smell that reminded her of sweet, green plants, and beneath that, something darker and seductively masculine. Gooseflesh that had nothing to do with cold flashed down Ella's arms and legs.

Stealing to the doorway of the sitting room, she saw Rodan lounging on a couch of sea foam green. He was facing away from her, reading, apparently, holding the book as if it were priceless against his bare torso. It hadn't been the carpet making him appear blue; his skin truly *was* blue, a pale, silvery shade that naturally made her think of clean, cold water. The sight of him was so delicious that she blurted out a request without preamble.

"I want you to kiss me," Ella demanded.

He started and looked over his shoulder. "Good gods," he exclaimed, scrambling off the couch and dropping his book. Ella thought it had some rather ridiculous cover on it, in which the woman was dressed in precious little and the man in even less. Then she remembered that the man in front of her wore nothing but trousers, and she wore only her underclothes.

"Little minx, what do you mean by barging in here?" He stood and composed himself–which meant he leaned against the doorframe with one well-muscled forearm. Ella tore her eyes away from the lean stomach muscles that led invitingly–scandalously– down into his trousers.

She cleared her throat. "I already said. I want you to kiss me."

He dropped his arm and scrubbed a hand across his face. "And I told you, I don't seduce virgins."

"I am not asking to be seduced," Ella said, stepping forward. This felt different than their first encounter. Last time, she had been vulnerable and confused, and then curious about the slow-kindling fire in her belly. This time, she may have felt a bit nervous, but it was nothing compared to her determination–or to said slow-kindling fire.

"I have nothing to pay you with," she added, "but I do not need–er, all of your services. I am just asking for a kiss. Surely, we can find some kind of suitable exchange for that?"

"Why? I'm flattered, of course–I'm easily flattered. Hazard of the job. But surely there are half a dozen village boys lining up to offer you their lips. And probably a bit more," he added grimly, with a sudden darkening of his countenance that Ella found oddly thrilling.

Ella let her gaze roam the comfortable room. How to explain this? Simply, as always. "A most undesirable person has asked me to marry him," she started, "although demanded is more like it. He even claims to be skilled at love-making. Well, I suppose he's old enough to have learned something by now." Suppressing a shiver of disgust, she went on. "I don't want to marry him, naturally. But in the likelihood that I have no choice to refuse him, I do not wish my first kiss to be with him."

"Good gods." He exhaled and ran his hand across his face again, muttering, "what is it with you humans marrying young women off to corpses?"

Ella, ever the literal-minded, could not help but add, "he isn't quite *that* old," but with one step he stood before her, and suddenly literal descriptions did not matter.

"A kiss of your choosing is the least you deserve," he said. He had not touched her, yet Ella felt her skin burn as if he had traced his words across every inch of her body, and she felt quite breathless.

"So you will kiss me?" she said.

His eyes roamed her face and settled on her lips. "It will take some restraint to leave it at that, but yes. I will kiss you. Happily." He took the sleeve of her chemise between two fingers, which Ella vaguely registered had slipped down her arm. His hand brushed her skin as he slowly drew the fabric back up her shoulder.

"We have not agreed on payment," she whispered.

"True." He leaned closer until Ella bumped against the wall behind her, and Rodan whispered in her ear, "Consider this a gift, free of charge."

He braced his hands on either side of her, not touching her aside from the caress of his gaze on her skin. She could feel the warmth of his gaze like the warmth of his body so close to hers that one deep breath would bring them together. Unfortunately, Ella had forgotten how to do that.

"Tell me your name, darling," he said. "I'd like to know who has broken into my house after I told her to have a nice life on land."

"Ella. And I didn't break in. The door was open."

His low chuckle made her shiver. "Ella. A pretty name." He glanced appreciatively down at her bodice, making Ella feel as if he could see through it to the tender skin beneath.

"Well?" She breathed. "Did you change your mind? Are you going to kiss me or not? Don't you put your hands on me or something?"

His gaze snapped back to her face. Ella began to wonder if water spirits had the ability to make love without the use of their hands, and was alarmed to see an expression almost certainly of concern on his features.

"You really are an innocent, aren't you?" He exhaled slowly. "I'm not going to grope you. And no, love, I've not changed my mind, either. If this is to be your first, and likely only proper, kiss, then we will take it slowly."

Chapter 5

Ella was just about to protest that she did not have all day when he leaned down again and kissed her shoulder. Just a light brush of his lips. It sent tingles of pleasure through her like a jolt of warm lightning.

"Oh!" Despite the pleasure of it, her shoulders jumped to her ears in surprise.

"Too much?" Rodan murmured. Ella shook her head emphatically, thinking she heard a smile in his voice.

"Just lean into it, love. I'll go slowly." With one hand, he held her shoulder with aching gentleness, and began a trail of soft kisses up her neck until he reached the quivering pulse beneath her jaw. The tension in her muscles eased with each caress. "If you say stop, I will stop at once."

"I do not want you to stop," Ella gasped. She felt ravenous for something she could not name, something that involved feeling a lot more of his skin than just his mouth. Impulsively, she reached for his chest and pressed her palm to his smooth skin. Whereas he had felt cool last time, now he was deliciously warm.

"Oh," she said, "you feel delightful."

He, however, made a sound as if anticipating pain. In one swift movement he had captured both her hands and pressed them to the wall on either side of her.

"I said no hands yet." He kissed along her jaw.

"You said no groping." Ella gasped. "You never said that 'no hands' applied to me. And you are, in fact, holding me with your hands."

He grunted in frustration. "I should have said no talking, either." Withdrawing so that he met her eyes, Ella saw his pupils dilated and heat in his expression. *He is quite good at acting the part,* she thought. She opened her mouth to say so when instead his mouth claimed hers.

He tasted of salt and lust. Ella sagged against the wall, liquid with desire. His hands supported her, yet she wanted hers free to indulge in tangling her fingers in his hair and wrapping her arms around him. His kiss was delicious, it was dangerous, and Ella felt herself melt in the incandescent heat of it.

She made a sound of protest when he pulled away, but somehow the words, "thank you," escaped her lips. His lips were swollen, and still his eyes smoldered, as if he had enjoyed it as much as she had. He chuckled softly.

"How polite you are. It makes me want to do entirely impolite things to you, you know. Who are you, Ella, beneath your manners?" He removed a hand to bury it in her hair and draw her close as he lowered his lips to her neck again. Ella's released hand flew to grip his shoulder, trying to tug him closer. He laughed softly again. "Have no fear. I am not done with you yet."

When he returned to her lips, a whimper escaped her mouth. She struggled to free her other hand, and the moment he released it, she wrapped both arms around his neck just as she had wanted to. His kiss became rougher, deeper, but no less pleasurable; she gasped against his lips as his large hand seized her waist and drew her against him. Her attempts to return his kisses grew more confident, more urgent.

His grip on her waist tightened. She became aware of something hard pressed against her belly, but it only made her weaker in the knees. Desperately, she rocked her broad hips against him.

"Dear gods." The words ripped from him. He pulled away, his breathing as labored as hers. Ella reached for him, aching with hunger, but he gently lowered her hand to her side and stepped back, holding up his own hands as if in surrender.

"I think," Rodan said, struggling to catch his breath, "that is enough for now."

Ella walked—or rather, stumbled—along the shore of the pond. She felt swollen, throbbing, and tingling, enthralled by the memory of his body against hers, yet completely unsatisfied.

"Curse you," she murmured under her breath, casting one look over her shoulder. The surface showed no sign of him; he had disappeared swiftly, silently. "I wanted a kiss, and now I am less satisfied than before."

Evening bruised the sky purple. She slithered through her bedroom window, a ridiculous, drunken-looking grin on her face, hardly noticing her stepmother was already banging on the door. She almost forgot to be alarmed by the usual tirade of insults. Unfortunately, she did remember that her yellow dress was still at the bottom of the pond, safe in Rodan's home.

"Damn it," she said aloud.

"I *beg* your pardon?" Stepmother shrieked, in the tone of one who never begged for anything in her life. "Is this how you thank me, after all I've done for you? And what have you to say for yourself? Sir Edward is a patient man, but he was not happy when he left!"

Ella realized she had not been listening to stepmother at all. The memory of Sir Edward's proposal returned like a certain oily stain she could never quite remove from the best lace tablecloth.

With a thunderous bang her door swung open and stepmother entered, quaking with rage. Ella, frantically buttoning her gown, barely had time to register this new invasion of privacy before the woman began berating her, and this time there was no escape.

"You are ungrateful, Ella," she seethed. "Your father should have raised you better. I doubt even a real servant would have such poor manners as you! Sir Edward is returning tomorrow, and you will accept his generous proposal. The decision is final."

"But you did not ask me," Ella protested softly.

"Sir Edward is our nearest neighbor and owns the largest property in the county. Do you not see the benefit of such an alliance? Who else would marry you, girl?"

"I do not want to marry Sir Edward!"

Ella was not given to speaking loudly. The words burst from her with a force that surprised her as much as her stepmother. The older woman recovered from her surprise at this unusual outburst faster, a hatred hardening her expression.

"Very well," she hissed. "You will have to learn this sooner or later. A man can do things a woman cannot. He may be old, but he is strong, and should he take your maidenhood, you would be ruined goods. I would have no choice but to hand you over in marriage."

Ella understood the significance of her stepmother's words, as cloaked in euphemism as they were. A slow-boiling dread filled her. "Are you threatening me with rape?"

"Such things happen." Stepmother inhaled deeply and straightened her tall frame. "Now change at once and see to dinner. Let today teach you what should have been obvious from the start: what you want does not matter."

With that, Stepmother swept from the room. Ella slammed the door shut with all the force she could muster, but she could not shut out the bitter, clinging stain of violation.

Stepmother did not notice that Ella hadn't changed when she served dinner. The woman seemed content to barely acknowledge her existence, except to demand that the soup be warmed twice over. Ella ate the leftovers and cleaned up the dishes in the relative haven of the drafty kitchen. In bed, she tossed and turned for hours, troubled and jittery with fear.

The unrelenting night gave way to a pale dawn promising thick summer heat. Ella sat up, rubbing tired eyes, and looked at her one good dress hanging from its peg. What would a missing dress matter to Stepmother if Ella refused marriage again? What would it matter if Sir Edward had his way with her, one way or another? Ella rose and looked out her window. Her stepmother's words rang in her ears: *what you want does not matter*.

What do *I want?* Ella had never truly considered the question. In a corner of her heart there had always lived the desire to keep her home from falling to pieces; it was her beloved parents' home. It was home to her dearest memories of them. But complying with stepmother's demands had not kept the house intact. Nor had it kept Sir Edward's proposal away or his threat to her safety. Was anything truly hers to protect, or had it always been an illusion?

From the yard, the scrawny rooster crowed to greet the dawn. Soon stepmother would wake and demand breakfast. Ella found she was heartily sick of doing what she was told. In a world where opportunities for rebellion were sparse as frog hairs, the worn, much-mended dress suddenly seemed very important. Surely Rodan would tire of her, an ignorant intruder who did not pay, but he could not refuse to return what belonged to her. She would not need to stay longer than necessary. She only wanted a chance to speak with him once more. And, yes, memorize every mind-numbingly handsome detail of him, if she were perfectly honest with herself.

Ella pulled the pearl from beneath her pillow. She had stolen it yesterday, giving propriety the middle finger. It offered her a chance, an escape, however temporary. She looked at the pink dress on its peg and her stays lying draped over a chair. *Why bother?*

Dressed only in her night clothes, Ella climbed from her window and ran for the pond.

It would hurt nothing to ask for another kiss while I am there. If it makes me look desperate, well, I suppose I am.

Chapter 6

Rodan was not in the sitting room today. She found a kitchen through one door, very small and full of strange implements, but considerably tidier than she would have guessed. That left the darkened hallway leading from the sitting room. Before Ella mustered the courage to investigate it, a peal of feminine laughter rang from that vicinity. Jealousy flared within Ella's chest. *Naturally, he would be with a, er—client at this hour*. But the thought only served to remind her that nothing was wholly hers. What Rodan had shared with her was not unique to him. He had kissed many people. He had experienced an intimacy with them she would never know, whereas they, satisfied and well aware of his terms of services, had paid him generously in return. Ella tugged self-consciously at her threadbare nightgown, which made her feel ridiculous and humiliating, as the woman on the other side of the door likely had on even less.

The bedroom door opened and a voluptuous woman in a silken robe stepped out. Ella could not help staring. She was older, maybe even her stepmother's age, with long, tousled blonde hair and eyes heavy with sated desire. The robe slipped, exposing one of her large breasts.

"Oh my." Catching sight of Ella, the woman's red lips tugged into a smile. "I didn't realize he accepted charity cases."

Ella's cheeks burned with shame. "I am here for my dress, not charity."

The woman purred, sauntering around Ella as if eyeing a poor specimen of embroidery. "Well, he does like all types. Even the lower types, I suppose. But you're a young, pretty thing. You should enjoy yourself, pet. I always do."

She tightened her robe and sauntered from the room. *Without even a proper dress!* Ella heard the door open and shut, imagining the woman swimming gracefully to the surface, where no doubt a luxurious carriage and well-paid footmen took her home to a house that was not falling to pieces.

"Ridiculous," Ella huffed, though what she referred to remained a secret even from herself. *Maybe I should take my dress and go. I would be stupid to ask for another kiss.*

To fend off feelings of inadequacy, she began poking around the room. It was a masculine place. The blue-green sofas were all trimmed with dark wood in strong lines. She wondered if all water spirits dwelt in homes as comfortable as this. But the dress was gone from its place by the fire, and there were few places it might hide. Ella began examining a bookcase, which was full of titles resembling the book she had caught him reading last time, when a solitary book caught her eye.

It was a ledger book of some kind, and Ella flipped through it eagerly. Dates and lists of names of women and men told her this was a register of his clients. Her eyes shot to the most recent entry: a lady named Theodora Partridge of a well-known estate some miles away. A pen standing in an iridescent green ink pot sat next to the ledger. She seized it and wrote the date and her name in the line above with a flourish: Miss Ella Clement of High House. *There,* she thought as she shut the book. *I may never see him again, but I have left my mark.*

"I admire your tenacity," came a low male voice behind her, "but please do not steal my things."

Ella spun around, heart pounding. He stood close, but not close enough to hinder a full view of him. Rodan was entirely naked.

It was, for Ella, an altogether new experience. *No amount of sheep copulation could prepare me for this!*

"Oh," she said, staring. "I wasn't stealing anything," she protested, and stared again. His skin bore the faint blue shimmer that highlighted every muscle. *Well, that makes perfect sense, as he is a water spirit and water looks blue, unless it's stormy and then it is grey, though I've heard the sea sometimes looks green, too, but I already knew he was blue and oh my, I'd no idea he would look quite so* like that. Her mind was babbling, trying not to stare and failing as the seconds stretched taut. Rather like the man's—

"Please put my pen away," he said. An entirely wicked smile spread across his face. "You are making me jealous."

Ella realized she was stroking it in a fumbling sort of way, and hastily returned the long, slim instrument, nearly dropping twice it in the process.

"I came for my dress," she said, trying to ignore the warmth in her cheeks and the way her voice sounded far too breathless.

"Pity." He frowned, but his eyes were teasing. "I'd far rather you came for me." As if gripped by a spasm, with a groan he scrunched his handsome face and rubbed a hand violently over his features. Ella feared he would develop some kind of skin condition if this behavior continued. He muttered a curse, plucked a robe from a nearby hook, and wrapped himself in the fabric. It shimmered black and iridescent blue like water on a starless night. It also did little to disguise his rather excited state. This was odd, as the last time she had noticed his hard excitement, they had been pressed together and kissing passionately. *Maybe he is very fond of this robe.*

"Your dress is here." Without waiting for her to follow, Rodan opened a door in the hallway to reveal a closet full of clothes. All of them were the same size of shirts and trousers and masculine in style. Her pale, yellow dress was the only feminine garment among them. For some reason, this surprised her. *Miss Theodora Partridge doesn't leave her dresses here, then.* She felt smug at the thought.

Rather than offer her the dress, Rodan tucked it under one arm and tapped his chin.

"What I do not understand," he said, ignoring her protest, "is why you would come back for such a poor dress as this. Is it magical?"

"It's my only other dress," she said between gritted teeth. "Now give it to me."

He complied silently, but the way he regarded her, with something like pity, made her skin prickle. "I am not a charity case," she snapped.

"No, you are not." He sounded entirely sincere. In the silence that followed, Ella's empty stomach complained loudly.

"I should leave," she said, but he swept between her and the door.

"I should offer you a meal," he said. "It's only proper."

Ella eyed him skeptically. "You might have a client soon."

"I do not."

He was strange, Ella decided, and it was convenient to focus on that rather than on how happy she was to remain this strange underwater home a little longer. He made her feel almost wanted. She sank down on the sea green sofa and tried not to squeal with delight at the plump softness of it. Through the kitchen door, she could see Rodan busy gathering items. At one point he ignited a green flame, the light gilding his features. His beauty took her breath away. And yet for all his otherworldliness, as he went about his task he looked like an ordinary man in an ordinary kitchen—although, truth be told, even her father had never set foot in the kitchen that she could recall. Watching Rodan engaged in this domestic task made her ache with a longing for something simple yet far out of reach.

"I do hope you enjoy eggs," he said. Ella heard something sizzle as a pleasant, familiar fragrance greeted her. "Yes, chicken eggs. I work up quite the appetite in some of my visitors. They tend to turn up their noses at water spirit food." He gave her a roguish smile that made her quite hate these visitors.

"Have you always lived here?" Ella ventured. "I never knew you were here. Don't spirits lived in the sea?"

His face darkened suddenly, the seductive mischief turned to wary coldness. Ella shut her mouth, worried.

"We live anywhere and everywhere there is water. I thought humans knew that." The playful smile returned. He brought a plate heaped with scrambled eggs and handed it to her. It smelled delicious, redolent of herbs she recognized from her own garden. But one bite proved to be better than anything she had ever made in her dilapidated kitchen. She devoured it quickly, looking up to find Rodan watching her with a broad smile on his face. Heat flooded her cheeks.

"I shouldn't have eaten so quickly," she said. "But it was so good." *Slow down*, said her stepmother's voice. *No wonder you're so stout. Your father indulged you entirely too much. Greedy, selfish girl!*

Ella had inherited her mother's curves. Stepmother, tall and slim as a reed, seemed determined to point out this difference between them at every turn. Ella pushed the plate onto a small table with legs made of woven reeds, feeling as if a stone had settled inside her stomach.

"What's this?" Rodan asked gently. "Did it turn your stomach, love?"

Ella shook her head. Rodan sat next to her.

"You are exquisite, you know," he said. "And please don't be one of those women who refuses to accept a genuine compliment. Your curves are luscious. Why, the women in my village would love to be as healthy and plump as you are." His smile was a little sad.

That sadness on top of such compliments landed like the proverbial final straw. Tears spilled down Ella's cheeks. Rodan looked appalled as she stumbled through an apology, looking down at her lap when she was no longer able to look at him.

"Stop this," he said, even more softly than before, and gently turned her face to him. His fingers were light on her skin. "Apologize for nothing here. Tears are nothing more than a reminder that we all belong to the sea."

Ella knew herself lost in that moment. Never mind that he was spirit; never mind that he lived underwater in a preposterous, comfortable house; never mind that he made love to more people than she had seen in the past year. She didn't care about any of that. Much of her life had been spent resigning her dreams to the dust heap. There was no time for impossible things in a house devoid of love and full of demands, but here, she let herself feel the warmth of this impossible realization. *Do I love him?* Well, it was perhaps a bit early to say so. But she held onto the warm, shy feeling in her bosom. She would keep it quietly to herself, savoring it like a treasure, no matter whether he could return her feelings or not.

"All your visitors must fall in love with you," she said wistfully.

"No, darling." Rodan stroked her face once, brushing away a tear with the tenderness of a water lily petal. "They want my body, my skills. That is all I have to offer. You must remember that." He rose and took her plate to the kitchen.

Chapter 7

It is *all I have to offer.*

Rodan reminded himself of this as he scrubbed the dish clean. He wanted to offer her so much more. Oh, yes, he wanted to bed her, wanted to bring her to pleasure and to see her body arch and tremble through the throes of passion, but he wanted more than that. He found the idea of offering his services and sending her home repulsive. He wanted to spend all day with Ella. What did she love? What did she hate? What would it be like to wake up beside her tomorrow, and the next day, and on and on? What would it take to coax her from this timidity and who in all the mortal world had made her crawl into herself, instead of allowing her to claim everything that rightly belonged to her?

I am the last person to speak of claiming what belongs to oneself, he thought darkly. There was nothing to be done for it. He finished drying the dish—an odd gesture in this odd house—and tried to compose his thoughts.

When he returned, her brown eyes swam with tears again.

"Why won't you make love to me?" She asked.

Yes, why? His brain and other parts of him demanded to know as he gazed at this lush, rosy woman and her round eyes looking at him beseechingly. So much for his composure. Strangling a groan half of longing, half of frustration, Rodan managed to choke out, "I beg your pardon?"

"I may be inexperienced, but I know what I want." She brushed fingers across her eyes and straightened. The tears had gone, replaced by determination bruised with a desperation borne of frequent experience with denial. "There must be something I can offer for payment. I—I can continue cleaning out the stream, I can bring you more chicken eggs—please, I know I sound ridiculous. I am. Ridiculous, that is." She inhaled sharply, pressing her full lips into a line. Her eyes dropped. "Never mind. I should go. You've been more than kind."

Something like anger flared in his chest, not at her, not even at himself, but at this whole rotten situation and the people behind it. He did not want to be merely kind to Ella. He wanted to share so much more than that with her, and for so much longer than a single morning. He wanted her; she made it clear she wanted him. *Can't I give her that much?*

Rodan's hand shot out and grabbed her shoulder just as she turned away. The feel of her skin through her chemise offered him his own chance to feel desperate, a chance he seized and swam off into the sunset with.

"If I tell you the payment," he said, his voice rough in his ears, "you must decide whether it is worth your while. Please promise me you will not,

on any account, decide before thinking it over."
He drew her back until she gazed up at him, her
lips softly parted, her eyes calling him like sirens.
He dreaded this. He wished he could ask for
anything else but this. Ella's softness clung to him,
pulling at him. He had no choice in the kind of
payment required, but he owed her the truth.

"Your life," he said. "You must offer me a day
of your life."

Ella's forehead puckered in confusion. "How
so?" She asked. "A day of work? A day—with you?"
Pink stained her cheeks at the question. "That
sounds as though making love and the payment
are one and the same."

"No. But gods, Ella, I wish it were." He shook
his head. "I take a day of your life, quite literally.
However many days fate has allotted to you before
we met, when you leave my bed, you will have one
less in your future. These terms I do not control
but must abide by them."

He could see her thinking about it, which
brought him a strange relief. Most people agreed
without batting an eye. Apparently, the last tenant
of this cottage had had a reputation, or perhaps it
was the tales humans told one another that led
them here. Either way, people found him and
knew what they wanted. Most came to him
because their lives were unbearable in some way—
boredom, an unhappy marriage, disappointment,
grief. What was one less day of an unbearable
existence if they could spend a few hours in
forgetfulness?

"You may have it," Ella replied, returning him to the present. Her eyes remained large and serious. "I want you to make love to me."

"What makes you so adamant?" He couldn't help asking, and he was more than curious. She looked as if she were entering a serious legal contract. He wanted to hear her reasons for accepting this cost, as if she would say she wanted *him* and not simply the experience he offered. Which, he reminded himself, was ridiculous. *Of course she wants the experience. I just told her it was all I had to offer.*

"Because everyone else has made decisions for me," she answered. "Because I have always followed the rules, and it has not made my life pleasant, only bearable. I want to choose something for myself." She stopped with a little shake of her head. "I am sorry, Rodan. Of course, if you simply do not wish to make love to me, I– well."

She stammered to a halt, a blush suffusing her face, and she looked so charming that strange things happened to his heart. Not-so-strange things happened to his southerly regions as well. No one ever asked if he wanted to; they just searched him out and paid him. It was as if she saw him as a living person and not just a thing. He drew a deep breath.

"Remember what I said last we met? That I wanted to do impolite things to you? I was not lying, love." He gazed at her, wishing he could convey what those things were by gazing only; if he said them out loud, he might shock or frighten her. *Best to go slowly*. It would not be difficult to treat her with the utmost care, only difficult to remember this was not something far more intimate than a service rendered at her request.

"Oh. Well, that is why I'm here." Ella cleared her throat and brushed the hair from her shoulder distractedly, then looked at him with her eyebrows raised. "How will you take a day from my life? I would like to get that over with first."

"Come here." Rodan held out his hand. He had thought to do this afterwards, but Ella was right; better to get it over with now. At the touch of her hand in his, something shattered within him; he felt as if this were his first time being intimate with anyone, as if something new were about to happen and change him forever, as if this human creature was about to strip him bare, find all his vulnerable places, and kiss them one by one. The look on her face was trusting, if a little nervous, and he promised silently that he would give her an experience worth a whole month of days. As long as he did not break into a million pieces first.

The dark bedroom flickered with soft blue lights, like water dancing across the ceiling. Ella's eyes landed on a large bed neatly made. Rodan murmured something she barely heard about clean bedclothes. From somewhere came the sound of ocean waves. It was a soothing sound, which, despite her eagerness to proceed, she was very grateful for.

"Lie down, darling," said Rodan. Ella did so, staring up at the lights above as the blood pounded in her ears. He stood over her, his skin shimmering, the outline of his broad shoulders visible and his eyes catching the light.

"You are so beautiful," he breathed.

Ella's eyes threatened to spring with tears again. He sounded so unguarded, as if his words were not rehearsed. To distract herself she voiced an honest question. "Will it hurt? Taking a day of my life."

He knelt and leaned against the bed. "No. But it will feel strange."

When she nodded, Rodan reached into a drawer and withdrew a tiny bottle bearing a faint design and uncorked it. "Just close your eyes. Remember, you need only lie still."

Ella nodded, murmuring assent, and settled into the cool pillows. She heard him speak, but his voice had changed; no longer did he speak in liquid tones, but in a harsh, grating sound. His fingers brushed her temples.

Ella gasped. A searing light blazed across her vision, leaving her strangely breathless; she was shaking. Her eyes flew open to find Rodan watching her intently. The light was gone. Rodan held her hand and stroked it softly, giving her time to recover.

"How do you feel?"

"I'm fine," she said. "Just a little dizzy. Is that all? Can we start now?"

"You're sure? That was a quick recovery."

"Yes, I am sure," she said, huffing in frustration. Rodan bowed his head and exhaled. He seemed oddly relieved, as if he had expected much worse from the exchange. When he lifted his face to meet her gaze, a wicked, mischievous smile drew across his face.

"Seeing as I have your express consent, we shall commence with impolite things."

He leaned over her and touched his lips to hers. The softness of his kiss sent waves of surprise and longing flooding through her body.

She had expected him to be swift and rough, judging by his expression and his words. This kiss made her want to weep from his tenderness. The way his lips brushed hers, the way he cupped her face with both his hands, offered a care that melted her core all the faster for its unexpectedness. A fire burned brighter within her. As with their first kiss, he was intent on drawing out her exquisite agony, teasing her with brief caresses on her lips and tongue and face.

She was sitting up at this point, using one arm to keep herself from falling over and grasping him with the other, when he rose to sit beside her on the bed.

"I am not sure what to do," she whispered.

"What if I do what I do best," he said between kisses, "and you tell me if you want me to stop or repeat the action? Is that amenable?"

Ella, quite happily losing her faculties of speech, responded with "Umhm," and a nod of her head. And then inhaled as the backs of Rodan's fingers slid down her throat and grazed the skin between her breasts. Just one slow, teasing stroke, and then he withdrew his hand and unbuttoned her nightgown slowly. He held her gaze with an expression that she half expected to set fire to her chemise. Leaving the nightgown to fall open, he instead palmed her breasts through the fabric. Her face—her everything—grew impossibly hot and hungry. Hunger was the only way to describe it. He seemed to take an unbearably long time with each caress, and she tried to tell him, but forming words was impossible. Whatever odd sound she managed seemed to do the trick. With his breath hot on her neck, Rodan slid the fabric down her shoulders until it pooled around her hips.

Goodness, she was naked before him, or as good as, and it didn't feel wrong in the least. When he cupped her breasts with his hands, kissing down until he reached the fluttering of her heart, Ella's head fell back and she clutched at his shoulders to stay upright.

"Good gods, Ella," he whispered against her skin. "Is it improper to say that you are exquisite? To worship you with my body? Because words are insufficient."

He was looking up at her with something akin to awe, and it stroked Ella's inflamed senses, a pleasant ache to add to all the others. She wasn't nearly naked enough. She wanted his hands everywhere. Urgently, she tugged off the thin gown and tossed it on the floor.

Chapter 8

Rodan uttered a surprised oath as she lay back against the bed, fully bared to him. The flush spreading from her chest to her face made him nearly dizzy, and her soft, swelling curves made him mad with desire. "Not that I mind, darling," he said, his voice strained, "but I wasn't expecting you to undress at once."

Her eyes, heavy and curious, filled with uncertainty. Her hands rose to her throat, brushing her skin as if she was deciding whether or not to cover herself.

"Do you want to stop?" He asked, fearing more than anything to cause her harm.

"No." She shook her head, sending ripples through her blonde hair. Even her voice was enough to drive a man to pieces. "But I–I am not used to being naked. I know this isn't supposed to be proper, but this feels even less so."

"I'd have you naked every day if I could," he said, noting with pleasure as the flush deepened and a shy smile tugged at her lips. He decided it was time she spoke less if he could help it.

Ella welcomed his mouth on hers. When their kisses had grown longer, more desperate, and his hands roamed more of her body, he pulled back, eliciting a wordless complaint from her lips.

"I'm going to touch you, darling," he said against her mouth, "here, see?" And Ella bit back a whimper as he stroked her in secret places, nodding emphatically *yes, yes,* and *yes.* Her voice escaped in little bursts until she was making the most immodest sounds. Warm wetness slid down her legs and he slipped a finger inside her. *What is that—how does he!* Ella's thoughts shushed themselves as Rodan's fingers moved in ways she would have to ask him about—*later!*—

Ella arched into the swiftly building sensation. She cried out, flooded with a pulsing ecstasy that overtook her and dragged her along in its inexorable wake.

"Well done, Ella darling." Rodan sounded triumphant. He kissed her softly, taking a moment as her breathing returned to normal and her body calmed. "Tell me if this next part is good, all right?" And he entered her slowly. Ella's gasps came from deeper within her at the feel of him between her throbbing legs, smooth skin buried in tender heat. A deep groan escaped him. His voice sounded strained, and Ella wasn't sure what to make of it.

"Does it hurt, love?" He drew back to search her face.

Assured by his expression that he was enjoying this, she responded, "it's a little uncomfortable. No. Don't stop," she panted when he began to withdraw. "Don't leave."

He grinned. "It isn't too improper for you?"

In response, Ella managed a frown at him. "Stop asking me that," she said breathlessly, and even pretended to be annoyed when he ducked his head to hide the laugh she saw threatening to escape.

He kept still while she adjusted her position and the first discomfort eased into something that made her eyes flutter shut. A breathy moan escaped her lips. Rodan's fingers found her again; sensation grew, swelled, and transformed the discomfort into hunger, ravenous and deep. He slid into her fully. Her eyes flew open and she pressed against him, giving into her own rhythmic rocking.

"Say my name, Ella," he whispered roughly in her ear. "When I make you sing again, I want my name on your lips." She could only moan her agreement. Goodness, was it possible to experience that burst of pleasure more than once? The first time had unmade and pieced her back together. Now, full of him and this new sensation, she clung to Rodan, a lifeline in an overwhelming tide, and something in his movements changed. Gathering her to him with one arm, he thrust repeatedly deeper, faster, until she clenched and trembled and cried out for him, and he groaned, pulsed, and stilled.

She lay panting as Rodan rolled to one side and tucked her against him. A feeling like floating suffused her body, but she struggled to adequately describe it to herself. *Making love is the most delightful*—no, that was hardly it. The smell of Rodan's skin next to hers, the sound of his breath slowing gradually soothed her senses. It felt as though every nerve in her body had been washed clean, wrung out, and left to dry in the sun, tingling with warmth and happiness. "I shall never look at laundry the same way again," she said, and laughed in wonder.

"No one has ever laughed when I've finished with them," said Rodan, propping his head up. He was trying to regain his mischievous smile, but the effect was rather lost on account of his languid, sleepy gaze. "Or discussed laundry. Should I be concerned?"

"No." She snuggled into his side. Content, for a moment, to pretend they were the only people to lie in this bed, to feel his smooth, well-muscled arm around her. Then her eyes shot open.

"Oh dear," she said, thinking of all the costs she had been warned spirits could extract from unwary humans. "I allowed a spirit to be the death of me after all—but only a little."

"Only a little?" Rodan murmured. Maybe it was Ella's imagination, but he looked vaguely perturbed. "You do have a way with words."

"I had no way with words earlier, thanks to you." She blushed again, which seemed ridiculous when she was starkly aware of the firm length of his body pressed against her naked side. He had seen her bare and called her beautiful. She had climbed to peaks of pleasure unimaginable that left her vulnerable and powerful, and he had been there for all of it. And if he'd done so because she had paid him to do it, well. His tenderness was real enough to make up for the loss of one day. She found it well worth the cost.

Lost in a languid haze, she let her mind wander as her eyes roamed over Rodan's body. Still feeling unaccustomed to the male form, she found him beautiful and intriguing. And unlike his earlier claim that his body was all he had to offer, there was so much more to him than that. She wanted to understand him. She could not let him go without asking questions, without trying to gather as clear a picture of him as possible to store for later.

"Why do you respond the way you do when I mention the sea?" She asked.

Rodan relaxed onto his back and placed on arm behind his head. She saw flashes of a storm in his eyes. For a moment she worried she had probed too much.

"It hardly matters," he answered.

"I don't think so. It matters to you, at least. That is not nothing."

He was silent a moment, perhaps lost in the storm, his hand stroking her side. But then the waters soothed and his eyes calmed. "Water spirits lived in a village in the sea, near a cliff. It was my home." The pull of his voice was like the pull of the tide, the lilting tone of a hidden story revealing itself with each crashing wave. "The humans near the sea were intent on cutting the land into pieces, so they drew up fences and claimed the land for themselves. Some wanted the land beneath the water, too."

The storm returned to his eyes, and Ella felt an answering sadness. Rodan's thoughts were far away from the bed and their warm, entwined bodies.

"I was ensnared. Taken and brought to this pond. The last pond guardians left, or died, or were killed; I don't know. But I am forced to extract a harsh payment from anyone who finds me. I take people's lives, Ella, if only a day at a time."

"Oh Rodan," Ella murmured. "How terrible."

"I was foolish." His eyes flashed with anger. "Promises were made. I listened. Curiosity should not be rewarded."

"Curiosity is not always bad." Defensiveness prickled in her chest, for herself and for Rodan. He glanced at her in surprise, as if he had forgotten she was there. "I mean that you could not have seen through their lies."

"Could I not have?"

"No. I am sorry, but I would rather speak straightforwardly. Rodan, this is not your fault." Stepmother, and others, had chided her for lacking the flowery verbiage expected of the upper classes. Perhaps Rodan would find that tiresome about her, as well.

His hand stilled at her side. "Straightforwardness is an admirable quality of yours," he said, and Ella could detect no irony or teasing in his voice. "And to honor it, I must speak

57

plainly. You must go, Ella. This is no place for you. Go home and find someone who will love you."

I only want you, Ella thought; but she could never say that. She hardly knew him, and he did not really care for her. So instead she said, "I only want someone who will care enough to help me keep my home from collapsing," and immediately regretted the words, fearing they were insensitive to Rodan's plight. But he said nothing, only waited patiently for her to dress—which was rather difficult when her limbs felt like floating water weeds—and, instead of sending her on her own, swam with her to the surface. She rested her head beneath his chin and watched the waters brighten around them as they rose to the surface.

Impulsively, she kissed him. He returned her fervor. They floated in the cool water, her body already aching to wrap herself around him and welcome him in again. But he lifted her out of the pond and set her on the bank, rising head and shoulders above the water. Grey edged his blue skin, and Ella clutched at his hands in alarm.

"Find someone who will love you," he repeated, weak-voiced, and smiled sadly. "You deserve to be loved. Forget about me. Do not look for me again."

When he sank into the water, his skin flashed blue. Then he was gone.

There was no pearl waiting in her hand.

The cottage was dismal without her. Rodan knew he wouldn't be able to look at his bed without remembering her in it, without remembering her softest, most secret places and how it felt to lie with her. She was everything he'd hoped she would be. He would have regretted the whole thing if it weren't for how maddeningly delicious she was. And he allowed himself a measure of pride for how well he'd pleasured her. All his days, he'd be proud of the fact that she was so satisfied by his own hands.

I miss her already. And I can never have her again.

Rodan busied himself with household tasks, readying for the next client, trying to achieve the impossible goal of pushing her from his mind.

It's for the best. But gods, I hate it with every drop of blood in my body.

Chapter 9

Ella walked home in a daze. It was midmorning, and Stepmother would be furious when she returned. She hardly cared. Her limbs felt heavy on land, weighed down not merely by her wet clothes, but with the newness of what she'd shared with Rodan and the finality of their departure. She clung to the first, trying to ignore the second for a few precious seconds. *So, this is love-making.* She wrapped her arms around herself, smiling. It wasn't a burdensome feeling. It was soft and luxurious and free.

But Rodan wouldn't see her again.

She stopped walking, the wonderful feeling turning heavy and bitter as his last words rang in her head. *Forget about me,* he'd said. How *could* she forget him? The memory of their intimacy was etched into her skin and bones. He was a part of her now. Was she a part of him, too?

Forget about me.

I cannot.

But she could no longer ignore the future, either.

I will refuse Sir Edward to his face. It would be foolish, but it was the only choice she could stomach. Stepmother could hardly cast her from the house when she needed her to do all the labor. The woman would make her life miserable, but hadn't she always? The village was near enough; it was time Ella made an effort to form connections. Maybe she could find a respectable farmer or even another servant who would see how hardworking she was and offer her a marriage that would suit them both. She could convince herself that she did not need love in a suitable match; she only needed to survive. And the house was beyond saving. She should have seen that long ago.

"I am sorry, Mother," she said aloud to the stone building that had been her only home. "I am sorry, Father. I cannot hope to restore it any longer. I find I no longer wish to."

Wet clothes and all, Ella strode through the front door and heard Stepmother's voice from in the parlor. The grating tones of Sir Edward responded. They both glanced at Ella when she entered, varying degrees of surprise and anger on their faces as conversation died away.

"Sir Edward, how convenient," Ella said, her voice trembling only a little. "I have something to say. I will not marry you. You needn't continue your visits, unless, of course, you change your mind about my stepmother. Stepmother, I am weary of myself. I am tired of allowing you to bully me. I will continue working here, but you will not enter my room again. Now if you'll excuse me, I must change. Good day."

It took Stepmother less than a second to recover her voice. "Just one moment!" She cried, storming after Ella in a rustle of satin. "You impertinent churl! After all I have done for you. You have no idea of what Sir Edward offers! Do you really think that I would allow us to remain in this hovel when the gentleman has graciously offered us a place to live in his estate? You will marry him, Ella, and you shall never speak to me in that way again!"

Ella stopped in the hallway. "As far as I am concerned, Stepmother, you need never speak to me at all," she said. "I know my way around the kitchen and laundry well enough. You will not suffer any more than you already do."

A hand seized her arm and spun her around so that she came face-to-face with Sir Edward. He did not seem so ridiculous anymore. A keen light kindled in his eyes as he leered at her, lifting her arm to sniff at the sleeve. Her skin crawled in revulsion.

"Pond water. She has been to see a water spirit, baronetess. And if I am not mistaken, she has given her virtue to the monster."

Stepmother gasped and clutched at her throat in a passable impression of someone who cared about her stepdaughter. Ella tugged her arm in Sir Edward's grip.

"Let me go," she hissed.

"Oh, dear girl." Sir Edward chuckled, his grip tightening. "So innocent, but not as innocent as I should like! I think it's time we paid a visit to this pond. Someone has taken something of mine. And I do hate it when that happens."

Sir Edward dragged her from the house with Stepmother on their heels. Ella fought to stand upright.

"Let me go!" She shouted. If she was to be treated this way, she decided, it was time to shove propriety where sunshine never shone, and did so. Sir Edward doubled over with the impact.

Unfortunately, he did not let her go. Wheezing and red-faced, he only staggered onward, her arm pained by his grip. *He is not going to stop,* Ella thought desperately. *But if I struggle less, I can use my strength elsewhere.*

"Don't say I didn't tell you," harrumphed Stepmother as Ella allowed herself to be led. The sun was high and hot; Ella's half-dried clothes clung to her in a warm, damp mess. Soon they were all panting in the heat. The pond came into view at the edge of the woods, the unshaded part of it sparkling like a half-moon. Sir Edward, wiping a hand across his greasy face, released Ella and twisted a ring on his smallest finger. The design of it looked faintly familiar.

"Answer your master," he commanded. Ella was about to protest that *he* was no one's master when the water bubbled and roiled.

Hardly noting Stepmother's shriek, Ella watched in horror as Rodan rose to the churning surface. The pond broke and streamed from his hair, clothes, and skin as he climbed ashore, lurching towards them as if he had no control over his movements. The grey pallor of his face worsened when he saw Ella, and fear and anger flashed across his features. His mouth tightened in a thin line.

"No!" Ella cried.

"You've taken something of mine, boy." Sir Edward sounded delighted, rocking back on his heels. "It's time for my payment."

"Your payment is wrong." Rodan struggled as if caught in invisible bonds.

"I am not speaking of those little bottles." Sir Edward drew close until he stood nose to nose with the spirit. "You have ruined my future bride. But one bad turn deserves another. She will be mine, and you will continue guarding this place as long as I command it."

"Keep Ella out of this." Pale fury washed Rodan's features, which grew more corpse-like with every minute. "Fight me if you will. You don't deserve her."

"You cannot determine that, my fine fellow. You have been a most disobedient guardian." He reached to twist the ring on his finger—and slumped to the ground.

Ella stood clutching a heavy stone behind him, her chest heaving. Ignoring Stepmother's hysterics, she dropped her makeshift weapon and rushed to pull one of Rodan's arms around her shoulders.

"I quite like you fierce," he said faintly. "But it's no good, love." With that, he collapsed against Ella, sending them both sprawling to earth.

Ella struggled upright and tried to shove him towards the pond. His skin was cold, clammy, and deathly white. "We must get you into the pond," she panted. "Just get in the water, Rodan!"

He tried to shove her hands away. "Little minx, you don't understand. Sir Edward's claim on me will last as long as he survives. I am bound to him. You are the one in danger here."

Ella had pushed Rodan close enough to the pond that one of his legs dangled in the water. "I do not understand," she grunted, continuing her efforts.

"He forces me to take a day from each client, which he takes for himself and thus prolongs his life." Rodan's other leg landed in the water. "My life belongs to him. Get yourself away, Ella. Now!"

Ella paused for an internal battle with herself. Rodan couldn't struggle much longer. If only she could–

The stone lay next to Sir Edward's prone form and a frantic plan took shape.

She *could*, in fact. She could indeed.

Ella darted towards the unconscious man.

"Ella?" Rodan gasped.

"Ella!" Stepmother shrieked.

Sir Edward did not wake when Ella tugged the ring off his finger with much difficulty. *It bears the same pattern as the bottles, as I suspected.* He did not wake up as she searched in the reeds and along the stream until she found what she was looking for: another large stone.

On a hunch, she sprinkled some water from the pond onto the first stone and placed the ring on it.

"Trust me," she pleaded with Rodan, who watched her with wide eyes. Then she brought the second stone down on the ring with all her might.

It shattered.

From the pond rose a host of grey, misty shapes that filled the air and dissipated like smoke; Ella sucked in a breath as something cold entered her chest. Blinded and dizzy, she heard a scream as a sudden wind whipped at her hair and clothes.

Just as suddenly the air cleared and her sight returned. Where Sir Edward had been lay the shriveled husk of a man, swallowed in crumpled clothing.

He would never wake again.

In the shock, all Ella knew was that he must not pollute her beloved stream and pond. Gingerly, she pulled the remains away from the water and rolled them into some tall weeds. Little heaps of dust lay scattered in her wake. *I will bury this later.* Then she turned to find that Stepmother had fainted, her nose saluting the sky.

The only sign of her water spirit were faint ripples on the pond.

Chapter 10

Rodan drew in great gulps of water until his vision came into focus. Had it really happened? Was he truly free of Sir Edward's control? The missing weight of the binding magic, making him feel as light as plankton in a current, said it was so. He circled and dove, spinning through the water with an energy he'd forgotten used to be his. He hardly knew what to do with himself. There was his home in the sea, of course, the place that would always have a part of him. He would visit as soon as the autumn rains allowed for travel. But in the meantime?

In the meantime, Ella.

He stopped his acrobatics, suspended, his hair swirling around his head. He could not simply push her from his mind and body. Ever since he had sat with her on his sofa, he knew he was in a fast way falling in love with her. Such a declaration seemed premature, even though she made him feel bold and tender at the same time.

Yet he had nothing of value to offer her. After all she had been through, Ella could hardly wish to cast her lot in with a water spirit. Why should a human choose a life in the water, bound to another, especially when she had just escaped an unwanted marriage?

He paused for an internal battle with himself. If he saw her again, he feared he might do something foolish such as propose marriage–or at least a good bedding or five. The poor young woman had survived enough. Better to leave her and let her move on.

She saved your life, he thought. She deserved his thanks, at the very least. Deserting her without a word was a far cry from allowing her space to make her own life. And besides, it was highly improper for him to disappear without so much as acknowledging her services. He grinned at the thought and swam upward, this time of his own free will.

Ella was surprised, enraptured, and enraged, all in the time it took for Rodan to appear out of the water.

"Rodan! No, stop! Why have you left the pond again?"

His skin faded to grey as he skirted the horizontal baronetess and stumbled towards her, but his eyes were bright. *Oh dear,* thought Ella. *What have I done? Has air exposure turned him mad?*

"Hello, love," he said, a ghost of a mischievous smile on his face. "I did fancy you'd be happier to see me."

Ella could not help herself. She wasn't sure why he had returned, but the relief she felt compelled her to do something not entirely within the bounds of good manners. *Too late for that!*

Rodan rocked backwards with the force of her arms thrown about him. He chuckled weakly in surprise, then wrapped her in his arms.

"Is it proper to thank someone for committing murder?"

"Oh no." Ella withdrew and looked up at him. "I have, haven't I? I didn't think it would kill him! And the worst part is, I don't believe I feel sorry for it. Though that might come later."

Rodan swayed on his feet. One look at his grey face told her what to do. It was easy to bring them to the water's edge.

"I do not feel sorry for this," she said, throwing herself and Rodan into the pond.

She was quite proud of herself for not losing consciousness this time. Her lungs burned painfully as Rodan, regaining strength, swam down quickly, threw the door open, and flung them through the bubble of cool air into the entry way.

"You little minx!" Rodan caught her and kept her from falling, looking her up and down as if checking for injuries. "You could have drowned!"

"But you haven't thanked me yet," she protested.

He thanked her thoroughly until she went weak in the knees. This was the kiss she had expected, hot and desperate. He cradled the back of her neck as if fearing she would try to escape

him, which she certainly had no intention of,
while his other hand wrapped around her waist.
She broke away to struggle out of her clothes.

"I–care for you, Rodan." The buttons were
vanquished, with his enthusiastic aid. "I am not
asking for favors. But I find myself in search of
new lodgings." She gasped as he searched between
her legs and found that some of her clothes were
wet again, and for entirely different reasons. "I say
nothing of love or obligation. But as I can provide
you with chicken eggs and a clear stream, I
propose that we–Rodan!"

"The only stream I am interested in right now
is between your legs, and your clothes are in the
way." His attention deserted her thighs. "Ella. Did
you say that you care for me?"

"Yes."

"That is most inconvenient, as I care for you,
too. Note that I also did not say love."

"Noted."

"Love takes more time than we have had the
pleasure of sharing."

"Exactly."

"So, we shall settle on tearing your clothes off,
making love, which is an odd euphemism now
that I think of it, and discuss living
arrangements–"

"Rodan, darling, you can stop talking now,"
Ella breathed, and moments later they had
finished the first thing on his list and made a good
start on the second, without ever reaching the
bedroom. Pleasure grew within her, and her eyes
shut as a wave of ecstasy carried her to its peak.

"Do you know," she said afterwards as she floated blissfully down from said peak, lying with Rodan on the sea foam green sofa, "I believe propriety is a lie meant to keep people from really good things."

Rodan laughed, the first sound of pure delight she had ever heard him utter.

Epilogue

Shafts of light danced in the water's depths, illuminating swathes of waving plants in shades of blue and green and silver. Ella smiled and spun, savoring the water's caress on her skin. "I am so glad you are feeling better," she said to the pond, and, tucking her bundle snuggly under her arm, swam towards home.

She had finished tidying the stream only a few days ago, but the water was already crystalline. Shimmering schools of fish darted across her path. Near the surface, she had seen strands of late frog spawn swaying like ropes of fairy lights. Her parents would have been delighted.

She found living under the pond surface delightful. Indeed, she was in danger of overusing the word, but it was the best she could think of to describe her new life. The pearls which Rodan gave her for underwater breathing were made of transformed morning dew. He could make an endless supply for her. She learned to swim, to grow plants underwater, which Rodan helped her to harvest and cooked himself, and to hold her breath long enough to swim to the surface without a pearl. The first thing they had done was to find that all the bottles in Rodan's possession were, in fact, empty.

"But Rodan," she had asked him after this discovery, "why sex?"

He shot her a look both surprised and amused. "Why did I bed all those people? Sir Edward told me to kill anyone who wandered onto his property. He never demanded a specific type of death. I chose *le petit mort*."

"I suppose he never noticed you only took a single day instead of their whole lives," Ella had mused.

Rodan had laughed. "I shall be eternally grateful for this failure of his."

He never admitted another client from then on.

She found him harvesting a patch of water plants as she arrived. He glanced up and sent her a grin that still made her blush.

"Ella, darling." He finished tying the bundle to keep them from floating away and kissed her, stroked her flowing hair, which had loosened in her descent. "How was the village?"

"Quite busy. And I heard the most fascinating news. Apparently, my stepmother now lives in Sir Edward's estate."

"However did the good lady achieve such luxury? Certainly not by stooping to deceit!" Rodan's eyes widened in exaggerated surprise. Ella had grown accustomed to his expressions and felt a smile tugging her own lips. "And how, pray tell, did she manage that?"

"I am not sure. But the word is she married him before his tragic passing, and now lives the life she's always wanted as his widow."

"How lucky for her." Rodan's voice was grim.

Ella, upon hearing the news, had immediately wondered how the woman had convinced the authorities of her supposed marriage, and if she enjoyed ordering numerous servants around as much as she had enjoyed ordering around one stepdaughter. Perhaps those numerous servants would prove less malleable than she had been, but she would never know.

She held up the bundle. "This is the last of the chicken eggs," she said. "One of the Romani families my stepmother so feared has taken up residence in the house. They have even begun repairs. It belongs to them now."

"Does that bother you terribly?"

"No. I have a home. Without Sir Edward, they should be able to live there unmolested. And there's a certain poetic justice to it that I cannot help but delight in."

Rodan smiled, pulling her close and kissing her. Ella sighed and kissed him back.

"Rodan," she murmured, "as much as I love playing in the water, there is nothing better than lying in bed with you. Or," she continued as he trailed kisses down her jaw and memories of recent events replayed themselves in her mind, "on the rug, or sofa, or standing up against a wall."

"Agreed." He was doing things that made Ella appreciate her floating state, as her knees might

have buckled had they stood on solid ground.
Rodan tugged her towards the cottage.

"We might try all of them," Ella murmured, to
which Rodan also agreed, and they set about
doing just that.

THE END

Thank You

Thank you to my wonderful ARC readers, who helped spread the word in such short notice! Brandi, Elaine, Beth, Melissa, Holly, Jessica, Ari, Kathryn, and Jennifer, I'm so grateful for you and your help.

More from Riona Beck

About the Author

Riona Beck used to hate romance novels, until she realized that the real problems were patriarchy and purity culture. Among others...

When Riona began to see that her hang-ups around this particular genre were protective measures she no longer needed, she discovered how much she actually liked kissy, sexy books. She even decided to start writing and publishing romance stories for real.

While she loves a good plot and adores character friendships, and is constantly analyzing the ways in which the world of romance sometimes upholds harmful narratives, you can always find her working on her next feel-good, serotonin-delivering story full of banter, chemistry, and kissing. And yes, sex.